Pete *the* Sheep-Sheep

by Jackie French

Illustrated by Bruce Whatley

Clarion Books • New York

Clarion Books

a Houghton Mifflin Company imprint

215 Park Avenue South, New York, NY 10003

Text copyright © 2004 by Jackie French

Illustrations copyright © 2004 by Farmhouse Illustration Company Pty Limited

First published in Australia in 2004 as *Pete the Sheep* by Angus & Robertson,

an imprint of HarperCollins*Publishers* Pty Limited. First American edition, 2005.

The illustrations were executed in watercolor and colored pencil.

The text was set in 22-point Berkeley Book.

www.houghtonmifflinbooks.com

Printed in China.

Library of Congress Cataloging-in-Publication Data

French, Jackie.

Pete the sheep-sheep / Jackie French ; illustrated by Bruce Whatley.

p. cm.

Summary: The sheep-shearers in Shaggy Gully all have a sheep dog, but the new guy Shaun uses an extremely polite sheep named Pete.

ISBN 0-618-56862-X

[1. Sheep-shearing—Fiction. 2. Sheep—Fiction. 3. Sheep dogs—Fiction. 4. Dogs—Fiction. 5. Humorous stories.] I. Whatley, Bruce, ill.

II. Title

PZ7.F88903Pe 2005

[E]—dc22

2004030935

ISBN-13: 978-0-618-56862-8

ISBN-10: 0-618-56862-X

10 9 8 7 6 5 4 3 2 1

To Dunmore, a sheep among sheep

— J.F.

To Phoebe, a dog among sheep

— B.W.

Ratso, Big Bob, and Bungo sheared sheep in Shaggy Gully.

Ratso had a sheep
dog named Brute.

Big Bob had a sheep dog
named Tiny.

Bungo had a sheep dog
named Fang.

grrrrrrrr!

But the
new shearer
had a...

...sheep-*sheep!*

"Hi, I'm Shaun," he said, "and this is Pete."

"Baa!" said Pete politely, which in sheep talk means, "Delighted to meet you, gentlemen. Madam, please follow me, and Shaun will attend to you shortly."

6

"You can't have
a sheep-sheep!"
cried Big Bob.

"You need a
proper sheep
dog!" yelled
Ratso.

"Strewth!" muttered
Bungo, who never
said much.

"Pete's as good as any
sheep dog," said Shaun.
"We just do things…
differently."

"*Baa baa!*"

said Pete,
which in sheep talk means,
"Thank you for waiting, sir. Shaun will be right with you."

9

Shaun and Pete were a great team.
Shaun was a sensational shearer,
and Pete was so polite that the
sheep would follow him anywhere.

"Baa baa?"

Pete would ask.

"Yes, you're right," Shaun
would say. "I do need to take
off a little more around the ears."

"That's not the way we do things here!"
yelled Ratso. "Go bring in some sheep, Brute!"
"Hurry up, Tiny!" called Big Bob.
"Yup," agreed Bungo, who never said much.

But the sheep didn't
move. They were
waiting for Pete.

woof!

grrrrrrr!

arf arff arfff!

11

"That sheep-sheep is nothing but a troublemaker!" yelled Ratso.

"He has to go!" cried Big Bob.

"Too right!" shouted Bungo, who never said much.

"If Pete goes, I go," said Shaun.

grrr

rrrr!

woof!

arf arff arfff!

"That suits us fine!"
yelled the other shearers.

13

"Now what am I going to do?" Shaun said sadly. "I love shearing sheep!"

"*Baaaaa!*" Pete pointed out.

"You're right, Pete," said Shaun. "At least I still have you to shear."

14

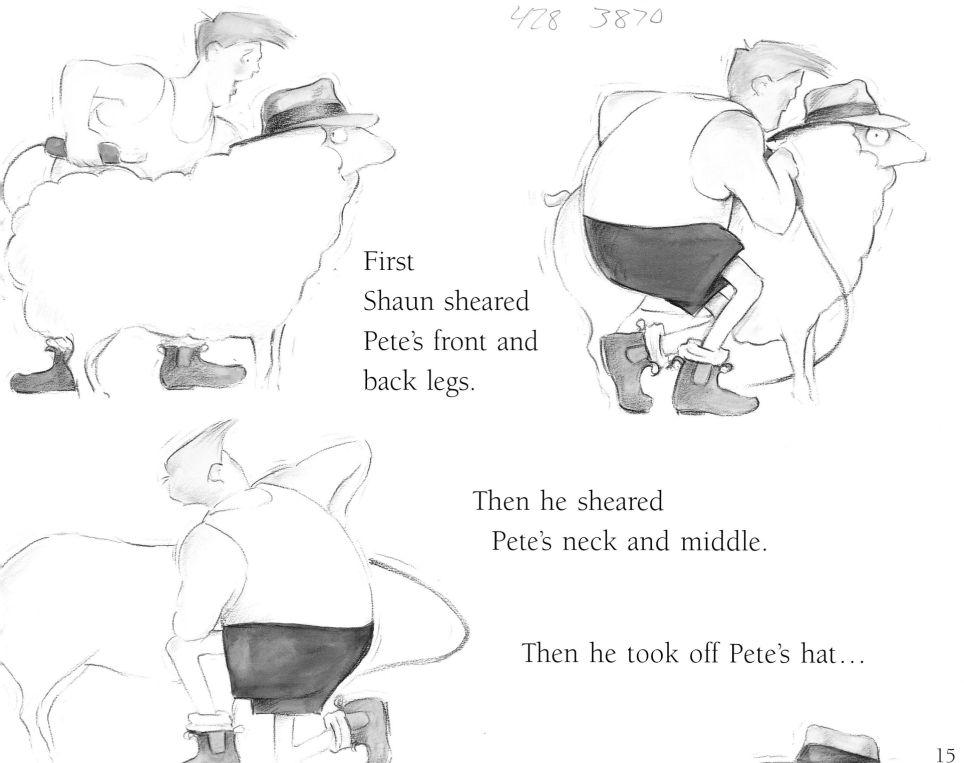

First
Shaun sheared
Pete's front and
back legs.

Then he sheared
Pete's neck and middle.

Then he took off Pete's hat...

15

...and gave him a whole new look!

When Pete showed it to the other
sheep, they were amazed.

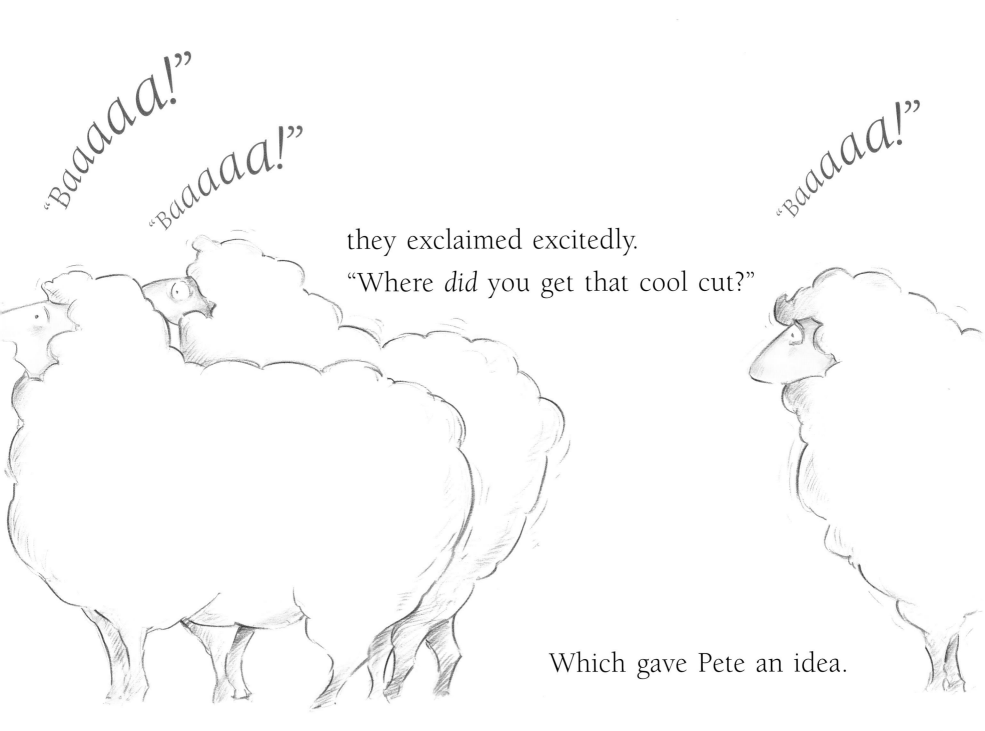

"Baaaaa!"

"Baaaaa!"

"Baaaaa!"

they exclaimed excitedly.
"Where *did* you get that cool cut?"

Which gave Pete an idea.

A week later, Shaun opened his own business.

Their first customer
was very happy.

So was the second.

And so was the third.

Soon, everyone was talking about

Shaun's Sheep Salon.

News of their success spread quickly.

Before long, Shaun and Pete had so many customers, they couldn't look after them all.

21

The other shearers were furious.

"It's not fair!" said Ratso. "*We're* the ones who have proper sheep dogs."

"Too right!" agreed Big Bob. He looked around. "By the way, where *are* our dogs?"

22

"Jumping jumbucks! Look what
I just found!" roared Bungo, which
was more than he usually said in a week.
The three shearers raced into town.

23

Meanwhile, their dogs were creeping sheepishly into the salon.

"*Woof?*" asked Brute hopefully.
"*Arf,*" agreed Tiny.
"*Grrrr,*" added Fang,
admiring a sheep Shaun
had just sheared.
"I'm really sorry,"
said Shaun,
"but our salon
is for sheep only."

"*Baa baa baaaaa!*"

said Pete.

24

Shaun grinned. "You're right, Pete," he said. "There's no reason why sheep dogs can't look gorgeous, too."

Shaun had just put Tiny under the hair dryer when the three shearers rushed through the door.

"Where's my dog, Brute?" yelled Ratso.

"Where's Tiny?" cried Big Bob.

"Fang!" bellowed Bungo.

"*Woof!*" barked Brute firmly.

"*Arf arff arfff!*" added Tiny.

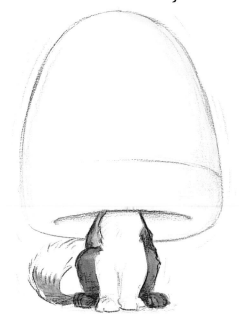

"*Grrr*," growled Fang, which in dog talk means, "No way am I leaving before I'm finished."

"What are we going to do now?" moaned Big Bob.
"There aren't any sheep left for us to shear."
"And our mangy mutts have deserted us," added Ratso.
"Doggone dogs," grumbled Bungo.

"*Baa baaaa!*" said Pete,

Shearers wanted

which in
sheep talk means,
"I have an idea."

In the end, it all worked out happily.
Ratso could shear sheep styles that
were almost as good as Shaun's.
Big Bob specialized in sheep dog styles.
And Bungo learned how to speak to the clients:
"Oh, madam, you do look lovely!
I only wish everyone could look
as gorgeous as you do!"

"Baa baaaa!"

said Pete, which in
sheep talk means,
"Everyone *can*
look gorgeous!"

29

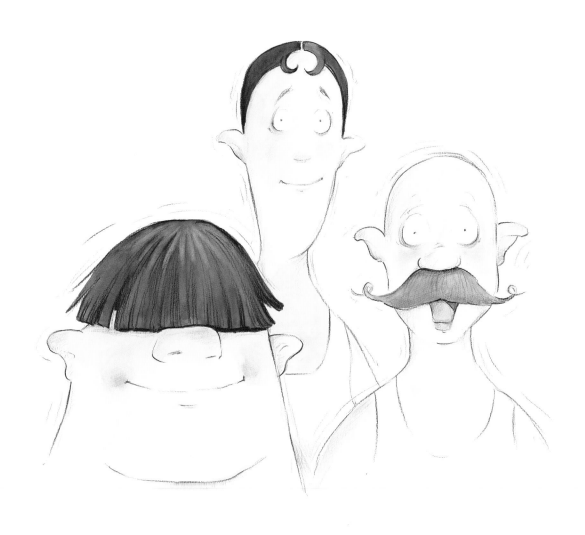

And after a session at Shaun's Animal Salon,
everyone did.